The Photo Album

Also By K. B. Dixon:

The Ingram Interview

A Painter's Life

Andrew (A to Z)

The Sum of His Syndromes

My Desk and I

The
Photo
Album

a novel

K. B. Dixon

3B
Baffling
Bay Books

Publisher: Baffling Bay Books

ISBN 978-1-7346759-4-8

1 3 5 7 9 10 8 6 4 2

For Sandra Jean

Introduction

This collection of photos is in a sense a memoir. It is the story of a photographer—a very amateur one: me—yours truly, the chronically conflicted Michael Quick. As you will soon discover when you turn the page, I am new to the medium—or, more accurately, I should say I am new to it again. I have flirted with photography both regularly and inconsequentially in the past, but as I suspect my expensive new camera will suggest, I seem to have gotten more serious about it lately.

One of the problems with getting serious (or semi-serious) about photography is that at some point in the process after you have mastered the various manuals and looked into the basics of making competent images, you will find yourself thinking more than you would like to about the subject of photography in general—about the recalcitrant mystery of it: what it is, what it should be, how it should best be done. It is grueling and ultimately profit-less, this noetic gum-chewing. The only thing I feel I can say with certainty right now about the camera is that there doesn't seem to be anything it cannot make interesting—a verity that is in equal parts both worrying and wonderful.

If you would like to jump over to Plate 4 and take a quick look, you will find a photo that is pretty typical of the sort of thing you can expect from me. I have for the most part eschewed the "art" shot as well as the emphatically vernacular one. I have taken a sort of middle way, a way in which there is no glory, but with which I am (at the moment anyway) comfortable.

K. B. DIXON

Plate 1

This is a photograph of my mother with her mother taken I don't know how many years back. It might not glow with the allegorical meaning of some, but still it fixes us. The women, elegantly dressed, sit primly side by side holding each other's hand. Just minutes before there was, I think, a violent argument from which my mother's mother has not backed down—an argument about the man who would one day soon become my father.

My mother and my mother's mother share the same mouth and the same slight build, but they do not look alike. The emphatic bulbousness of the older woman's head alludes phrenologically to the size of her impressive brain while the dourness of her expression suggests it has not been much of a comfort to her.

My mother, who wears her rings on nontraditional fingers, is clearly still very much interested in looking pretty. Her hairdo is complex—a small braid rings the center of the creation like a halo separating the severity of the center-parted bangs from the relative voluptuousness of the pompadoured crown. The dress—which is quite obviously silk—leaves her shoulders bare. And in her eye there is a girlish glint I do not recognize; a glint that disconcerts me; a glint in which one can see an intimation of the wildness that will one day overwhelm her.

Plate 2

The man on the left is my mother's mother's husband. He has been dead for a decade now. A business person of some repute, he was one of those go-getters who went and got. A man whose ethical compromises were thought to be fewer than those of the egregiously compromised norm, he was considered by many to be a representatively resplendent example of the top something-percent of his generation.

The taller, balder figure on the right (with his hand stuffed deep into his suit coat pocket) is James McBain. Not as much is known of him as should be. A silent partner in a number of my mother's mother's husband's enterprises, he is today something of a mystery.

If I were to give this picture a title, it would be something like "The Distinguished Conspirators."

Plate 3

I have never been an advocate of the "snapshot" aesthetic. I have some sympathy for it—especially insofar as it is a reaction to the contrived and airless alternative so popular with a certain downtown crowd—but I find most of these sorts of pictures interesting only as illustrations of a theory, a theory that seems to me conceived in desperation.

This particular shot is a bad one (disorganized, the focus uncertain, the highlights blown out) because I was in a hurry—not because I was trying to make some statement about the oppressive orthodoxy of traditionally-done "good" ones.

This bridge—whose name I do not remember—is wedged into a heavily-timbered hillside of the Coast Range. You cross it on the way to Cannon Beach where—if you time it right seasonally—you can find a remarkable breakfast of gingerbread waffles.

I bought a new lens—a wide-angle zoom. This is the second shot I took with it. I have included it here as a sort of salute to my equipment. I think I have for the most part avoided the obsession with gear that afflicts and addles so many of we dabblers. That does not mean, however, that I am entirely without envy or that I am above the occasional flaunting of whatever technical resources I may have at my disposal.

The man in this picture with the golf clubs is my neighbor, Thomas Lockhart. He is a lawyer. He specializes in getting drunk drivers back on the road—on getting them out of jail, getting their records expunged, getting their licenses back in their hands. This lens—a 12-24mm—is not considered a good one for portraiture because it tends to distort. I didn't care in this instance. I wasn't trying to flatter the man. What I wanted was a broad, environmental shot— a shot that recorded not just Tom but the conventional ostentatiousness of Tom's defining upper-middle-classness. (Note the convex profile of the status symbol parked on the periphery.)

Plate 5

Sometimes you are tired and you lie down but you do not go to sleep. Or you go to sleep, but awaken shortly for no apparent reason—no noise or rocking dream has startled you; you just wake up. You think about this, about not going to sleep, and you know it is not good for you—you know that thinking about it will keep you awake so you try to stop thinking about it. And, of course, you start thinking about that, about trying not to think about it. You have never once in your life stopped thinking about something you were thinking about because you thought you should, so you find yourself trying to remember the best advice in this situation—not only what it was, but who supplied it (so as to determine its worthwhileness). Was it best to get up and do something (like watch television) until you felt sleepy again or stay in bed resting however fitfully?

Tossing and turning—unable to retrieve any authoritative recommendation—you eventually get up, go into your office, sit down in a cold leather chair, and start to read one of the books you bought on taking better photographs. It starts off with all sorts of tips on flash photography which you can skip because you do not like flash photography and are going to stay away from it as much as you can. You take great pleasure in ignoring this information, in cavalierly flipping these pages unread—pages about stuff like softboxes and studio strobes. You wonder about your reaction to the guy who wrote this book: why are you inclined to dislike him when he is in so many essential ways simply harmless?

Do I find counsel?

Yes.

About what?

It is about shooting on cloudy days. Don't complain about a drab sky, he says, just keep it out of your picture. Wish novelists would do that with dull scenes and summaries.

As you can see above, my desk clock is quaintly analogue. The time—4:10—is of course Ante Meridian.

Plate 6

This picture was taken by my lovely wife, and I have included it as a rarity—not for its subject (or anything associated with its subject), but for its orientation. As a rule Amy shoots virtually all of her pictures on the horizontal. The horizontal is, of course, a natural bias with almost all photographers, but Amy has made this natural bias the foundation of her personal aesthetic, shooting a "skinny picture" only when compelled by an uncooperative form—like this Lodgepole Pine.

This is a photo of Luke Moore, a distant neighbor's missing son. It was taken in better days before he was transformed by adolescence into a considerably less attractive person. At the moment no one seems to know where Luke is. We think he has run away, but given the times we live in—with one sort of moral mutant or another lurking around almost every corner—we have not been able to ignore the possibility that something else might have happened.

K. B. DIXON

Plate 8

I don't know exactly what this small wooden carving is supposed to be—a toy, a crude knickknack, a model from some larger, more ambitious project. It was found wrapped in tissue paper in a trunk in my grandparents' attic and is assumed to have some sort of talismanic relation to a past that is of no interest to me. There is supposed to be some story attached to it—a heartwarming one of triumph over adversity, I believe—but no one seems to know who was supposed to remember it.

Plate 9

The above is a photo of our incorrigible daughter Kayla. She has a new boyfriend. His name is Phillip Wood. He is a recently graduated, stayed-in-school-way-too-long literature major. Right now he is working at Looking Glass Books—one of those small, selective places that cater to the liberally educated, the sort of shop you drop into if you are looking for a copy of *The Plague*. They met in the grocery store—Kayla stocking up for the week on oranges and bananas, Phillip on frozen dinners (spaghetti with meat sauce apparently a heavy favorite).

This is the first shot I took for my Portland, Inside and Out series. When I first got re-interested in photography (after I re-familiarized myself with certain technical issues and camera basics), I came up with a project to keep me shooting, to keep me interested and busy—a documentary sort of thing: Portland interiors and exteriors.

This particular gleaming men's room is hidden in a maze of hallways on the sixth floor of the new Fox Tower. You can, I think, feel the tiled chill, smell the citrus-scented air freshener.

This is a photo of my friend Ryan Richardson—a writer of postmodernist fiction. It was taken for his novel, *Trance*. Ryan was not an easy subject. He hated being stared at through a viewfinder for any length of time. He had impossible ideas. He wanted something that made him look like the sort of person who just might, on a good day, write the sort of book a certain sort of reader might want to read. He wanted something candid but ambiguous—something that would preserve his anonymity but at the same time bear at least a passing resemblance to reality (in the hope of suggesting to the most easily duped of us a minimal sort of reverence for the idea of truth).

Plate 12

This photo of Amy and me on Wallowa Lake was taken by the man who rented us the canoe. It was a beautiful day as you can see—windless, glassy. We had the lake to ourselves. It would have been a better picture if it had been shot from a different angle—lower and to the right—but it is not bad for your basic vacation snap. We look like we are having fun—and we were—but you can tell, I think, from the expression behind the smiles, the undercoating of apprehension, that we were novices, that we were in the boat but not of the boat (as the gilded explicator might have it).

Plate 13

Like many, I am attracted to the strange beauty of ruin-
ation, to the visceral effects of the peeling-paint picture.
My inclination is to prefer those that allude to a metaphysical rather than a sociological subject—pictures about loss,
decay, and the passing of time as opposed to those about
deprivation and injustice.

I took a picture of this telephone—which you see is now being used as a piece of decorative bric-a-brac—because it reminded me of the one that saw me through puberty, the phone I used regularly way back when—way back when actually "talking" to the people I knew (especially young women) seemed important. I remember an excruciating conversation with Annette Bogan. I remember trying to explain to her why I had not called back when I had left a message saying I would. I tried to find a gracious way of not telling her the truth—that I had not called back because I did not feel like it (I had not recovered sufficiently from the ordeal of our previous *tete-a*-tete)—but I was unsuccessful. I was not very good at that sort of thing, and Annette was hypersensitive—no nuance of language, logic, or tone ever went undetected or unexamined. I was fourteen and new to emotionally complicated relationships. I was confused and exhausted by them. What was the point of so much pointless torment. I was beginning to understand what I would not understand fully for quite some time—namely, that much of life was for me simply incomprehensible. The spirit here is, I think, retrospective.

Plate 15

I am a little wary of this shot. It is almost impossible to take a picture of a police car that is not immediately interpreted as political. This particular police car is parked out in front of Daniel Moore's house. (This was a week after Luke Moore was reported missing.) I don't think anyone in the neighborhood had ever seen a police car parked out in front of anyone's house before. It was a momentous thing—like a spaceship landing. It was bizarrely energizing—we felt like we had been awakened in the middle of something unusual and large, something infinitely more interesting than our regular everyday lives.

     K. B. DIXON

This photograph relies almost entirely on its context for its meaning. It does not seem to be of anything in particular, and I think that as a description this is accurate. Its subject is not the esoteric postmodernist one of subjectlessness, but a more common, everyday documentary one. This is not a picture of the mouse—this is a picture of the last place the mouse was seen. It is the picture of a place that now looms large in Amy's fertile imagination, the place her eye now travels to first when she walks in the door.

Style is a perennial problem in photography—that is, individual style. There isn't much room for it. One's choices in style—the varieties and variations—are severely limited by the medium, which is why "subject" almost invariably ends up becoming so important to the intrepid practitioner. It is much easier to make a subject your own than a style—down-and-out farmers, for example, or circus freaks. I have always had a thing for doorways. If I ever start taking photographs seriously, maybe this should be my signature subject.

The doorway above leads to the irrepressible Dr. Huffman's office. I have been thinking about going to see him, about renovating myself, about becoming a more normally social person. Tim Kramer has seen him and offered nothing but accolades, but this is as close as I have ever gotten—this long hallway, this door.

Plate 18

If I don't make doors my signature subject, maybe I'll make roads. Long and winding ones.

This particular example leads to the airport—that Stygian portal to the glamorous ordeal of travel.

Kayla and Phillip have been living together for a month and already there are signs of trouble. The other night Kayla wanted to talk to Phillip about her visit with our friendly GP, Dr. Lyon, but Phillip was too busy. The whole time she was trying to terrify him with stories of her cholesterol, he was underlining passages in *The Red Badge of Courage*.

I think you might agree that in this photo the sky is a little too blue. That is me—I did that. I was just getting back into photography when I took this picture, and, like most newbies, I was a little drunk on color saturation. It is easy to rationalize this sort of thing when you are inexperienced and your interest is solipsistically skewed in favor of a personalized expression.

Plate 21

I have included this ambiguous image in the hope of encouraging at least one seriously strained interpretation—the sort of thing I once thrived on as a college sophomore: the polysyllabic exercise of frivolous intellection, the anxiety-assuaging excursion into the syntactical backwaters of academic gobbledygook that purports to explain *how* a thing means rather than *what* it means. Something perhaps about invocation of an archetypical response to the creative imperatives of the elemental being—something where the sheer shinola level is noticeably high. An analysis perhaps of the photo as a poststructuralist critique of the problematized struggle for a transgressive interpretation of the construct fields surrounding certain iconographic ensembles and their tangential links to the heuristic evaluation of the primal image domain.

K. B. DIXON

I have no doubt that Katherine Lockhart—Tom's long-suffering wife—is an alcoholic. You can hide this for a while, but somewhere in your forties that invisible ink starts to makes its way to the surface. You can see it in the complexion, the set of the eyes, in the special species of suggestive sags, the preliminary transmogrification of the nose. Katherine tries to compensate, she tries to conceal the news of her affliction behind a show of oozing hospitality, but she never oozes enough to fully obscure your view of her underlying despair.

This struggle to seem affable has been hard on Katherine—it has taken a lot out of her, exhausted her. The stress, along with the drinking, has compromised her immune system. She always has a cold.

Plate 23

This picture is included not so much for its subject or its formal qualities as for its relationship to a fleeting sense I had of myself as a photographer. If you are going to get all serious about it—and I'm not sure that I think you should—a photograph is an admission by the photographer that however much he might prefer to equivocate, this is something he has found engaging. Both the eccentric and familiar qualities of this something provide an evaluative commentary.

As a rule I try to keep my postproduction manipulations of the image to a minimum. I will crop, I will adjust both white balance and color, I will sharpen, I will occasionally do a little burning and dodging—that is about it. I have never been able to fully equate technical manipulations with imaginative ones. I would say about half my photos are virtually untouched—like this table of tangerines.

Plate 25

This is a picture of one of those in-between places—those places that keep the interesting or significant places in Portland from bumping into one another. The ratio of places like this to the other sort is about 100 to 1. I've included this particular in-between place because it is the setting for Ryan Richardson's new novel. It is the coldness of the light, I think, that lends this characterless corner its nihilistic nuance. The shadow in the lower left that looks like simple vignetting is, in fact, a shadow cast by Ryan himself. He is standing off to the side surveying this model of his imaginary stage. He does not look happy. This book has been difficult, and his publisher—who was old to begin with, but who has only gotten older—no longer seems capable of feigning a nour-ishing interest in yet another marginal project.

Plate 26

I should apologize for this picture. It is difficult to respond to. It is a simple abstract that is not an abstract at all. I picked the spot I wanted and shot straight down. What looks like a flat, minimalist abstract, a simple study of straight lines and color, is, in fact, a parkscape detail. The yellow line is painted along the edge of the concrete walkway so people will not fall into the pond that occupies the top two-thirds of the picture. The water in this pond has been turned this unusual shade of green by algae. I have included this picture simply because I took it. Perversely enough, I enjoy taking these sorts of pictures considerably more than I enjoy looking at them. That is what I think of when I look at this—the thorny philosophical question. Also, I think of the boy who is off to my left terrorizing a flock of hapless ducks as his mother stares on passively. The scene makes me wonder what has become of basic moral instruction—it fills me with a fear for the future.

<h1 style="text-align:center">Plate 27</h1>

This is one of those candid photographs taken in a cafe of an unknown couple caught in the middle of what is obviously a serious conversation. I suspect from the mutual misery in their expressions that something between the two of them has changed and not for the better and that this intense and meandering discussion—which has been going on for a while now—has not helped, has not improved things or made them clearer.

I suspect the young lady—let's call her "Jessica"—has told the young man, "Kevin," that she wants him to be honest with her, but he knows this isn't true. What she wants is for him to explain himself in such a way as to make it possible for her to believe what she would prefer to believe about what seems to have happened. She wants him to explain his feelings, how they have changed and why.

Neither particularly likes having to hear what the other is saying although both are trying to be if not kind, at least not hurtful. Jessica thinks if she knows what has happened, what has gone wrong, she will be able to do something about it. Kevin has no such illusions.

When Jessica gets home tonight she will start calling her friends. She will discuss this conversation, the one she just had with Kevin. She and her friends will deconstruct and decode it—sift each sentence for a secret meaning. When

     K. B. DIXON

Kevin gets home he will turn on the television set. He will watch one of the late-night talk shows. He will laugh at a few of the better jokes in the opening monologue. He will listen listlessly to the dysphasic ditherings of an augmented young starlet as she effuses about her latest movie and the thrill of working with a cinematic legend like X, Y, or Z.

This shot of an unassuming brass table lamp is as emotion-ally neutral as I could make it. A simple statement of fact, I think of it as a sort of ode to representation—a comment on the banality of the phantasmagoric, on the changing image-landscape super-saturated as it is with computer-generated inventions where the fantastic has become a stale bore and the quotidian an endangered exotic. We bought this lamp at a small shop in Lake Oswego—Naomi's. We bought it to replace an expensive but god-awful piece of bric-a-brac that Amy had smuggled into the marriage—a kitschy thing with a Russian pedigree.

Plate 29

This is Katherine Lockhart and her troubled daughter Rachael. (Rachael was at one time romantically involved with Luke Moore, the boy who disappeared.) You can tell, I think, from Rachael's scowl that she takes no pleasure whatsoever in communicating with her mother. The ordeal of doing so has been ruinous. A consistently uncontained Katherine has crushed something essential in her. She is a creature of singular dexterity—Katherine. There is no moment she cannot or will not try to manipulate, no sentiment she will not season with reproach. There is with her always a sense of censure in the air. The one thing these two have in common—the tie that binds, however tenuously— is their poor opinion of Tom, the disappointing husband, the inadequate father.

I wish I had known what I was doing when I took this picture. If I had, I would have done a much better job. I would have gotten closer, filled the frame.

Phillip (upper right) has been getting together with a small group of literati. They are planning to launch a new quarterly—a thing tentatively titled *Flummoxed*. Kayla isn't happy. She thinks Alicia Wilkin, the woman who is putting up the money (and who will be the poetry editor), has designs on her cleft-chinned pencil-pusher.

Plate 32

The above reproduction of this photo is an image of an image. Because the photo itself is of another photo (of another image), the above reproduction becomes, in fact, an image of an image of an image of an image—in this case, a black and white image of my lovely wife in her transcendent teens scooping up in her arms like poker winnings a pair of wiggling moppets (her younger sisters, Anna and Allison). The allusion, of course, is to the idea of an infinite regress.

I don't remember exactly where or when I came across this chic little conceit, but it was infatuation at first sight. I don't remember finding it especially profound as an idea (whatever its relation to arguments involving a certain type of paradox), but I did find it entertaining. It was a magic trick at the end of a dull day—it was pulling a bright-white, self-replicating syllogism out of your hat, it was sawing a scantily-clad proposition in half.

I remember being thoroughly charmed by an anecdote featuring the idea. (It might have been in Stephen Hawking's *Brief History of Time*, but I think it was somewhere else.) As told, it involved a little old lady in tennis shoes. A famous professor (either Bertrand Russell or William James) was giving a public lecture on astronomy. He described the solar system in detail—how the earth orbited the sun and the

     K. B. DIXON

sun orbited the center of our galaxy. At the end of the lecture a little old lady sitting quietly at the back of the hall raised her hand and was called on. She told the professor that she had enjoyed the talk and that she had found it very interesting, but that basically nothing of what he had said had been true: the earth did not orbit the sun—it rested on the back of a giant tortoise. The professor paused for a moment then asked the little old lady what the tortoise was standing on. "That's easy," she said. "It's standing on the back of another tortoise."

Again the professor paused. "And what is *that* tortoise standing on?"

The little old lady smiled, "Very clever professor. I can see where you're going. You might as well save your breath—it's turtles all the way down."

I've always thought if I ever wrote a book, that would be its title: *Turtles All The Way Down*.

The clichés of beauty are irresistible. It is usually (although I have to concede not always) some sort of affectation to pretend otherwise.

K. B. DIXON

Plate 34

What sort of pictures do I take? No sort in particular. Mostly it seems a chaotic, random type of thing that is really beyond my structuring.

I would say in general that I stay away from both the sublime and the ridiculously ordinary—in part because they have both been so hopelessly overdone, but also because I have an obdurate predisposition to be mundanely suspicious of extremes. In the beginning when I did list in one direction or the other, it was, of course, more likely to be toward the sublime than toward the subtexturally encrusted antithesis, but lately this has changed. Exploring the quintessentially common is a tricky thing to do right—it requires greater foresight and additional technical expertise—but I have found myself getting more and more interested in trying it.

Dr. Huffman did wonders for Tim Kramer, but Katherine Lockhart, the woman jogging in the baby-pink track suit, has not been so lucky with Dr. Lawrence Lazott. She does not like him. She does not like his name—she thinks he should change it. She does not like the way he seems to encourage her hostility. She doesn't like where his office is located. She doesn't like the way he seems to only half-listen. She doesn't like his clumsy sense of humor. She doesn't like the things he says about her husband, the way he will occasionally defend the man's disapproval of her. She particularly doesn't like the boneless way he sits in his chair. She doesn't like the way he offers confusion where she thought he might offer hope.

Plate 36

This photo is from my early period when I was a little more fascinated with the power of simplicity than I am now, when I ignored the ornamental superfluosities that enrich a visual statement in favor of a stripped-down thing, a sort of formal extract. This was my second incarnation as a photographer. (My first, like most primitives, involved a fascination with color saturation. See Plate 20.)

I showed this photo to Raymond Marshall and Jennifer Holmes. I was interested to hear what they had to say. Apparently something about the way I presented it made them think they should try to analyze the thing. The interpretation they offered was otherworldly. I did not see at all what they said they saw. But then, they might not have either. They might have just been making it up to sound good.

In cahoots. Kayla had a long talk with her friend, Sarah (lower left, champagne-colored hair). She told Sarah about her suspicions of a liaison between Phillip and Alicia. Sarah didn't have anything particularly comforting to offer in response, but she thought it did Kayla good to hear herself saying some of the things she had been trying for so long not to say.

K. B. DIXON

Yes, a photo of Paris. How could I not have a number of them. This particular one was taken from the fifth floor of the Pompidou—the hill topped with Sacre Coeur, that famous whipped-cream cathedral, in the distance. Just landing in Paris raises one's IQ. No matter what you do, where you go, what you see or eat, or who you do or do not talk to, you will leave the place smarter than when you arrived.

I always wonder about the natives, the Parisians— their general attitude toward life. What is it? I suspect it is better than mine. Most people's attitude toward life is better than mine. The only people I know with attitudes like mine are homeless or clinically depressed. It is not the most appealing thing about me. Amy makes allowances. I have never known why, but I am grateful.

<h1 style="text-align:center">Plate 39</h1>

Since I have already included one picture of a tree (see Plate 6), I thought why not include another. Unlike the picture taken by my lovely wife, a picture I included for what you might call historic rather than thematic reasons, this one is all about the spectral associations swirling around its subject.

This particular tree (also, alas, a Lodgepole Pine) means a great deal to me. Standing starkly and inexplicably alone in the middle of a featureless meadow, this is an affecting shot, I think—an iconic image of isolation. I respond to this particular tree because it reminds me very much of the one I fell out of when I was ten. I broke both of my ankles. I had been up to that point an arboreal child—one who climbed freely. Now it seems I have become something of an acrophobe.

If this photo is a metaphor, it is a private one of my lost innocence, of my transformation with experience from young romantic to seasoned realist.

K. B. DIXON

Plate 40

This is a shot that calls out for a caption don't you think? Here are a few of the options offered by some attentive passers-by. Vote for your favorite. The winner will be announced next week at O'Connor's and will receive a signed (and framed) 16x24 archival print. Any resident of the U.S. or Canada aged eighteen or over should consider themselves eligible to enter.

> a. The mercilessness of mornings.
> b. Ragged silence.
> c. The devastating dimensions of summer.
> d. Heliophobia.

Plate 41

This is a picture of my desk drawer before I cleaned it out. It looks like some careless hoarder's idea of a time capsule—a cluttered shelf from Dr. Dementias's Cabinet of Curiosities. There are pens, pencils, postcards, programs, ticket stubs, reading glasses, grocery lists, pocket knives, wooden rulers, a heavy copper medallion with Samuel Johnson's face on it. If you look closely you can see part of a newspaper clipping sticking out from under that box of staples in the back corner. It is the second of only three stories I remember seeing in the paper about Luke Moore. (A missing sixteen-year-old boy does not get the same sort of attention a missing sixteen-year-old girl gets as the likelihood of the story turning out to have a suitably titillating sexual component is considerably reduced.) The article was about a ransom note sent to the Moores not long after the initial story of Luke's disappearance was reported. The note was a hoax. It was written by a pair of twelve-year-olds, one of whose brothers apparently knew Luke. There was also in this article a picture of Luke's girlfriend (the one after Rachael Lockhart)—a girl who it seems had an additional boyfriend, a disreputable type who, it was not so subtly suggested, might have been jealous and involved in something untoward.

     K. B. DIXON

Plate 42

This is another photo taken for my Portland, Inside and Out project. The subject is one of our colorfully disturbed street people. I have not taken many of these sorts of pictures because I cannot shake the feeling that they are exploitive. It would be silly to pretend that I do not find these marginalized people fascinating, but I am just not prepared very often to try this sort of thing. I have never been able to convince myself that I am doing it for the right reasons—that I am in some way providing an introductory service, embracing a difficult diversity, celebrating a broader view of humanity rather than simply trading on a prurient and callus curiosity. These people are easy subjects—they provide even the most mediocre photographer with credentials as a sophisticate, but these sorts of shots are not what they used to be. The elevating audacity was drained out of them decades ago. While I do think these sorts of pictures can make a valuable point about alienation, about isolation, about suffering, about the nature of the human condition, most of them don't. The respect repeatedly declared for the subject invariably seems more perfunctorily prescribed than sincere.

Plate 43

One of the things I like about this picture of a display window in a shopping mall is the feeling it prompts. When I look at it, I am transported—I am in this shopping mall, stressed and unhappy, trapped in the frigid, air-conditioned soulless-ness of the place. I want out. I like the emotional accuracy of the thing. I also like the 50% Off sign. (There are few things in this world more complexly ambiguous than a 50% Off sign. It invariably conjures simultaneously an even mix of excitement and despair.) And then, of course, there are the balloons. What can I say about them—they are like flowers. They are catnip to we who have for one reason or another sought to ignore the siren calls of nature photography.

I also like the reflection in the lower left corner of the young man seated across from the window. He looks like a legitimately serious person—a little overly proud of his profile perhaps, but otherwise resolute.

This room is where the writer, Ryan Richardson, gave his last public reading. He was here with a half dozen other local writers as part of a fundraiser for the University Press.

He never liked readings. He swore regularly after each that he would never give another; that he was not a performer; that if he were a performer, he would have gotten into something fun, glamorous, and lucrative—not literary fiction. The problem, he said, was inherent—it was not just with his invariably sad and distracting presentations, but with his material. It was better suited to private readings than public ones. It was unconventional not only in form and content, but dependent on a faintly resonating series of intracranial signals.

Plate 45

I would like to have included more photos of Amy like the one above, but we have a contract and I am lucky I have been able to include any at all. When it comes to pictures of ourselves, neither of us is usually ever very happy. We are not photogenic but rather phototoxic people. We would like to look better than we do in real life, but we usually end up looking anywhere from a little to a lot worse, which, when you factor in the contemporary viewer's natural inclination to make discounts based on a familiarity with the camera's ability to finesse the truth, can—and almost invariably does—end up producing an exaggeratedly appalling impression. So the contract. We have agreed with each other to veto rights—to complete, absolute, and irrevocable control over the printing, display, and continued megapixel-existence of any photograph taken by one or the other of us in which one or the other of us appears. We will save the brutal honesty for others.

Katherine Lockhart is, as you can see, one of those women who relies heavily on eyeliner. To me she looks like an angry, middle-aged Egyptian who has lived too long in Las Vegas.

She had a fling last year with Colin Ford, the man in charge of remodeling her kitchen. I overheard them talking together once. It sounded like they were discussing the work schedule, but they weren't. They were dancing linguistically around some arcane issue of their assignation. The air was thick with code, with alternative meanings—sophisticated in some classically scurrilous sort of way with Katherine coyly deploying a number of purposeful misunderstandings and Colin a similar number of vaguely masculine innuendos.

There was a party at the Kingston to celebrate the publication of *Flummoxed*, Issue #1. It was a nice looking piece of work. They used one of Scott Rudnick's grim collages for a cover. The thing itself—the magazine—was stuffed with reasonably good short stories (one about a political operative, another about sleep deprivation), essays ("Infinity and Me," "Visa Las Vegas"), and poems ("I have spent my evening/with a tumbler of antacid,/trying to forget/just a little of what I could not know;/and my night/with a syringe of formaldehyde,/dying to fit myself/into the smallest and darkest of places.").

Alicia Wilkin was there. She was svelte and groomed and confident in a country-club-belonging sort of way. I understand completely Kayla's worry.

Plate 48

One of the peculiar things about a photo is its afterlife. Photos are, as a rule, relatively quick and easy—quick and easy to take, quick and easy to take in. However good, one spends only a fraction of the time with a photograph that one spends with a painting. The irony, of course, is that the image (if not the feeling) may be more indelibly imprinted, may last longer. I have always felt that way about this photo. There is something in this woman's expression that stays with me—something that I am sure falls well within the purview of these newly-concocted algorithms that purport to measure image memorability but goes far beyond, deep into the psychic swamp of the treasured subjective response.

Plate 49

There was a desire early on at the Moore house to act as if nothing had happened, as if their son Luke had not, in fact, been reported missing. I know the feeling well. I often want nothing to be happening (more often than is probably wise to admit), but something always seems to be—for instance, in this shot that was taken in desperation as a sort of diversion from the ordeal of diversion. I had been conscripted against my will to oversee the semi-annual, hypoallergenic cleaning of our not-at-all-dirty carpets by a cadre of expensive professionals. The sharp focus here is on one of the machines being used to clean this carpet. With the dials, the metal tubes, the hoses—it could, I think, from this distance and angle, be mistaken easily for some sort of medical device. What I wanted, of course, was not to be distracted from what I was doing, not to be aggravated, not to have my attention divided like some cheap melon—but these wants were but whistles in the wind. The blurry figure in the background is Lewis Carr. He is a nice man, a sweet man, a harmless man, but he was here to run this particular machine and to talk to me incessantly about the amazing things his granddaughter did in school that week. He was not unreservedly welcomed.

Plate 50

This is a portrait of Jeff Tinter and his chicly distressed and be-stickered suitcase. He is one of those fidgety itinerants who is always going places, meeting people, having experiences. He is the sort of person Amy envies and who I feel I am expected to envy, but who, in fact, I habitually suspect of having some sort of psychological disorder. A serial obsessor perpetually on the run from boredom, he thinks of himself as a romantic figure, a modern-day maverick. I was once stuck in an elevator with him for almost two hours. He told me a whole lot more than I needed to know about Alaska.

I experienced this as an exquisitely beautiful scene—that is to say, the sort of thing one usually sees only in photographs—so I took the picture. We were in San Diego. We went to Balboa Park. I turned around and there was this mission steeple framed perfectly by palm trees and blooming hedges. If you were to say this picture was merely beautiful, I would agree with you. Like most people, I have seen too many beautiful photographs—I have become desensitized. This does not mean I do not want to see more or occasionally try to make one myself—I do. Does this make me a bourgeois?

Plate 52

The woman standing under the STOP sign is Carrie White. Amy knows her. She rents a room in the Lopate's house. She is an obsessive weather watcher—worried always about it getting too hot. She telephones Amy regularly, but she has nothing to say. She doesn't like living near the Moores (they are two houses down)—she is wary of an ambient misfortune—but she cannot afford to move away. Like many lonely people, she has an extremely complicated relationship with her television. She tries never to watch the news (which seems to her to deal mainly in destruction, duplicity, disease, and death) as it exacerbates an already exacerbated inclination to despair. She is always checking the time and feeling her forehead to see if she has a fever.

Plate 53

The next issue of *Flummoxed* is going to be devoted to the "Office Life." Phillip is writing a story for it. It is a story about a talismanic desk—a long, flat, heavy thing made of battleship steel—a desk almost identical to the one pictured above.

     K . B . D I X O N

Plate 54

I took this picture because of another picture—a picture I had seen I don't remember where, but had loved. I took it because it somehow seemed reminiscent, allusory, related in spirit to this distant recollection—the sort of picture that gives you that wonderful moment; that moment you cherished; the one you are always hoping to come across; the one that is in large part the reason you look at photographs in the first place; that intense, inexplicable experience of something captured and handed to you.

Brian Holcomb has a twenty-five-foot sailboat named *Baloney* that he keeps strapped to a dock in this marina. I don't know if he ever actually takes the thing out. Mostly it seems just for working on—a way to occupy the odd, empty weekend. A natural putterer, the pleasure for him seems to be not in the sailing, but in the getting ready to sail—in the cleaning, the scraping, the polishing of the bits and bobs, in the sharing of beers and bullshit with his fellow dabbling dilettantes. I think of marina pictures like these as the English accents of photography. They have an inherently unfair preemptive aesthetic advantage over non-marina pictures that is the optical equivalent of the inherently unfair preemptive auditory advantage the English-accented speaker has over the non-English-accented one.

<h1 style="text-align:center">Plate 56</h1>

The above photo is of a sign that miraculously appeared overnight in the Lockhart's front yard: "Fuller for Mayor." People in our neighborhood rarely go in for this sort of thing. Fuller—a small-minded, small-government conservative who stands for truth, justice, and the American way—is running against the unpopular, semi-disgraced incumbent, Tim McKinney. Ryan Richardson, my writer friend who is obsessed with political corruption in general and, in particular, with local political corruption, has collected a number of stories about Mr. Fuller, about skullduggery in the awarding of various sorts of contracts when he was an up-and-coming city commissioner. Ryan likes these sort of photos—photos where the subject is text, pictures you literally have to read. They appeal to his native sympathies. I like them too if the text is used as texture. I don't like them if the text is used as topic or theme—those sort of photos are for me simply posters or press releases.

Plate 57

I have a great respect for the idea of the "decisive moment," but I have never wanted a picture of anyone crying. One thing I have wanted though is a candid shot of Amy's "there-is-a-bug-in-the-bathroom" face. It is a fascinating thing that is almost impossible to describe—a comic mix of fear, disgust, and something else. Of course, I have resigned myself to never getting this picture. For one thing, the chances that I would be there at the "decisive moment" with my camera at the ready are virtually nonexistent. Even if I carefully staged it—surprised her with a rubber spider, for instance—it would not be a picture I was allowed to keep. (I refer here to "The Contract." See Plate 45.) For the time being I am making do with pictures like the above—a distant, almost-useless shot of Amy's not-entirely successful effort to remain expressionless when provoked. She is talking with the willowy Margret Pond, our local cat lady, and doing her best to appear both non-judgmental and non-nonplussed as she listens to Margret's spontaneous, logorrheic, and loopy disquisition on the ailurophobic myth of *Toxoplasma gondii* infections.

 K. B. DIXON

This looks like a carefully calibrated abstraction but it is, in fact, just an oddly angled (and telephotographically compressed) shot of a dramatically overlit stairwell. There is something uniquely attractive about the geometric form. There is a rightness and wrongness to it—a rectilinear precision—that is not present in the biomorphic form. As I have said, I indulge myself periodically. I enjoy taking these sort of pictures more than I enjoy looking at them (see Plate 26).They are usually of interest to me only briefly. I do not see them as intellectual or emotional communications—I see them simply as optical exercises and/or symbols of a cold and sanitary style.

I think of this as basically a science pic—a shot taken to study. This woman, Stacy Combs, claims to be a hypnotherapist. She claims that with a little abracadabra she can help you lose weight, quit smoking, defeat depression, improve your self-esteem, or get connected with one or more of your past lives. She is confoundingly ordinary-looking—normal, like the sort of person who would buy her floral-print blouses from Macy's, the sort of person who would have a tuna fish sandwich for lunch. One has to scan the image closely to spot the clues of callousness, to see there deep in the eyes—squatting behind that shallow smile—the clear and repellant intimation of the scheming parasite within.

I have included this shot for the atmosphere. It is a photo of what has been for a while now the most famous Italianate pile in Savannah—Mercer House, the site of a salacious society murder, the gothic, peeping-tom account of which became a bestseller (*Midnight In The Garden Of Good and Evil*) and a movie. It is a soggy picture. You can feel the weather, the humidity. You can smell and taste the moss. You can't have an idea in a place like this—you can have feelings, you can behave, but you can't think.

As an exercise in visceral recreation, it is related to the earlier (odorless) shopping-mall picture (see Plate #43).

Kayla told Sarah that she is thinking about leaving Phillip and that she had been dreaming regularly of attacking the poetry editor with a golf club. As always, Sarah tried to be supportive. She squeezed out probably a half-dozen different ways of looking at the situation—better ways—but Kayla was too far down in the dumps to fully appreciate the effort.

Plate 62

I like this simple little shot—this isolated sliver of reality that is normally overlooked. Teasing the meaning from apparent trivialities—it is one of the things that photography does so well. The more comfortable I get with the camera, the more inclined I am to rely on these sorts of spontaneous spasms.

Plate 63

It is not often these days that you have a chance to take a picture of someone with their horse. Usually it is someone with their car. This particular shot was taken in Hood River at the Apple Valley Store. Amy and I had driven up—as we do every year—to buy huckleberry jam, and there, standing out in front of the place, pig-tailed and sequined, was Rebecca Ellis and her pancake-colored horse, Gadget. I talked with Rebecca while Amy was in interrogating the jam-maker (and taste-testing pretty much everything in a jar). We talked mostly about cowboys. Rebecca understood them in a way I did not. For one thing, they were real to her. She did not find their hats surprising or whimsical.

This is a pretty straightforward piece of documentation—an uninflected shot of my fish tank, its glistening residents gliding about haphazardly but for a pair of yellow whatsits who seem to swim in formation. If I were interested in this photograph being considered a work of art, I would have had to deny the debt it owes to its subject. I would have had to insist on the primacy of a personal vision, claim that what has been presented is an esoteric interpretation of light and space or an expressive evocation of some sort of metaphysical mood. There is no idea more insidious, more responsible for crap pictures than the idea that mood or individual interpretation supersedes description. Description—which is at the heart of documentation—is at the heart of photography, and to cavalierly derogate it in favor of a self-aggrandizing aesthetic of visionary license seems to me simply wrong-headed and craven. The fear, of course, is that emphatic description will remind the viewer that the image is the product of a camera when the glory-hunting narcissist would prefer he think it wholly that of a rich imagination.

This is a photo of Catherine Mason. She lives several streets over from us and is always—as you see her here—out digging in her fussy garden. I think of this as a sort of ethnographic study. There seem to be any number of Catherine Masons in the surrounding neighborhoods—middle-aged, middle-class women obsessed with potting soil and time-release fertilizer.

Plate 66

I have no idea what the Moores have tried to imagine in their efforts not to imagine what was likely. I don't know either of them well enough. I have no sense of their thought processes, no estimate of how fantastical their scenarios might have gotten, how beyond reason were the reasons with which they comforted themselves. I don't think they believed their son Luke was safe, but they pretended to because it seemed to be what was expected of them by pretty much everyone.

<h1 align="center">Plate 67</h1>

Pictures of patterns and pictures showing motion—I am not a fan of either. I like taking pictures of patterns and do it fairly often, but, as with abstracts (see Plate 26), I don't much like looking at them—not for any length of time anyway. I find the remorseless homogeneity of these images initially comforting but ultimately oppressive—more a denigration of the individual and the authentic than a celebration of the many and the fecund.

This particular pattern-maniacal close-up is of a pot full of pearls. They are Amy's—hand-me-downs that are almost never worn, accessories better suited to an older neck and a dowdier disposition. There is a static quality to these sorts of pictures. The eye wanders aimlessly, lost, looking for direction and settling for rhythm and repetition. Obliquely lit, you can almost feel the cold smoothness of these beads at your fingertips.

I have reinforced the shot by getting in tight, by extending the echo of these symmetric contours to the edges of the frame, but what really makes this picture work the way it is supposed to work is that stray black pearl in the lower left—an earring, its mate missing and presumed ground to an iridescent powder by the ambitious filtration system that pasteurizes the Talbots' gizzard-shaped swimming pool. This contrasting element—this black pearl—in disturbing the pattern accentuates it.

Plate 68

For whom is this picture of a beautiful sunset still beautiful? The sunset itself still has the power to move you—it will make you bring the camera up to your eye—but the image, the image is exhausted. We have been sated and consequently desensitized—sated now jaded. There are strategies, of course, to address this problem—one is to employ the latest, greatest, most expensive new technology, to raise the standard sugar-level of the shot. Another is to obscure the issue stylistically, hide it in a marsh of formal monkeyshines—but neither is ultimately very satisfying.

Kayla misses the people who left with Phillip—the people he brought into the relationship. She also misses the books, the DVD collection, and the reliable transportation. Who is going to take out the garbage now? Who is going to get the mail, open the wine bottle, get stuff down from the top shelves, find the things she loses—keys, hats, scarves, sunglasses, etc., etc., etc.? Who is going to kill the whatever it is that is crawling?

<h1 style="text-align:center">Plate 70</h1>

This is a picture I took of Ryan Richardson's office. There is an arrangement to the dustless disorder that one senses rather than sees. The desk sitting at the center of this ambiguous ambience is a discarded teachers' model that Ryan rescued single-handedly from a surplus store twenty years ago. Covered with papers and mementos—small talismanic travel-trophies (a clay pot from Carmel, a marble pencil-holder from Florence, a wooden box from London)—its varnished flanks radiate a certain sort of retrograde authority. The sketches on the wall behind the desk are studies for a mural. They were done by a man named William Dyas Garnett.

I don't know how many times I have tried to get Ryan to speak at length about his writing—never with any success. I thought here in his padded lair might be the perfect place, but he was not inclined. He parried all my prompts. I can talk about photography, dazzle him with some malarkey about metering, try to lure him into revealing disquisitions, but he will not be lured. His writing is not something he feels comfortable discussing, he says—not even with himself. The most he will offer is a bland little bromide about experimenting with experimenting.

As you can see, this photo is not one of mine. It has been cut out of a newspaper. It is a three-quarters shot of a big-boned, poorly-groomed, and unexpressive Tamara Grimshaw. Thomas Lockhart is defending her. She has been charged with attempted murder. Intoxicated, she tried to run over her ex-husband. She crashed her car (an aged Toyota) into the side of a convenience store (see Plate 84).

K. B. DIXON

Plate 72

This dog belongs to the Jenners and is famous in our neighborhood for biting Craig Selby, the man behind last year's much maligned effort by the Homeowners Association to secure funding for a new community center. This is as close as I get to doing wildlife photography.

What can I say about the photo above—little really. Sometimes you are just interested in the light. Is that enough? It can be.

<h1 style="text-align:center">Plate 74</h1>

I love photography, but for all the hemming and hawing—institutional and academic—it remains a sort of peripheral art form. Those who insist most emphatically otherwise are not making claims for the medium but for themselves as practitioners. The above is a photo of a photo manufactured by Brian Burkholder. I say manufactured because... well, it was. A stew of appropriated images—pictures of snakes, teddy bears, taxidermied heads—it was cooked in a computer, not a camera.

Generally speaking, the harder one tries to make a photograph look like a work of the imagination, the easier one makes it to dismiss as a bona fide aesthetic artifact. There are exceptions, of course—lots of them. They are everywhere, like banana slugs. It doesn't mean anything. They don't prove the rule. Neither do they disprove it.

Is photography an art? I don't know. If it is, it is not one on a par with painting or sculpting or with the literary arts or the performing arts—except maybe dance. Maybe it is on a par with dance.

Plate 75

This is another shot for my Portland, Inside and Out series. We are, like every neighborhood, a neighborhood of freaks. This rust-dusted fire hydrant with the purple petunias planted about its base stands stoically at the southwest corner of Donald Fowler's doglegged drive. I think Donald is in some ways the neighborhood's freakiest freak. He is an astronomer, a person for whom the unfathomable vastness of the universe is a daily reality. No one likes running into him. He is a sort of walking slap in the face—a reminder of your unimportance, of your piddling place in the grand, intergalactic scheme of things. If by chance you find yourself in conversation with him, you will start to hear what you are saying in a way you would rather not—that is, you start to hear it in the way you imagine it must sound to him, as almost phantasmagorically trivial. What in your head started out as a perfectly fine pleasantry will turn quickly into a mocking bit of meaningless drivel. This is not Donald's fault. It has nothing to do with his general responses—which are invariably cordial—but everything to do with his simply being who and what he is, the dinner-plate-like face of cosmic insignificance.

I took this shot because I have always liked the beefy, macho-industrial shape of fire hydrants, but also because it has always seemed to me a peculiar thing to be associated

     K. B. D ixon

with Donald Fowler (even if only proximitously). Also, of course, there are the flowers. Someone—it had to be Mrs. Fowler—planted them. It fascinates me—the idea that she could, after all these years with Donald, still maintain an interest in flowers.

A halo surrounds this bowl of ice cream—a halo of meanings
and social constructs. What is it—ice cream? It is childhood.
It is a reward for good behavior. It is the felicitous emulsi-
fication of psychiatry—a scoop of cold security on a sugar
cone, a spoonful of well-being, a bowlful of therapy with
chocolate sauce, a pint of frosty anti-depressant, a musical
truck filled with good humor—purchased on a stick or in
cartoned ounces, not in fifty-minute hours. This particular
bowl is the equivalent of how many visits to the illustrious
Dr. Huffman? As the flavor here is Coffee Almond Fudge, I
would have to say a minimum of three.

It came as something of a surprise to me to discover how much I liked taking pictures of people working—or, to rephrase that (as per Dorothy Parker), how much I liked having taken pictures of people working. The actual doing of it—the searching for the right sort of people doing the right sort of work (chefs, for example), the wheedling for trust, the groveling for permission—is invariably a damaging ordeal, a quagmire of legal concerns, thematic issues, and neurotic sweat. The images though—if you can get them right—can be counted as a more-than-fair compensation.

Kayla bought herself a puppy. She has named him Omar. She speaks to him constantly in Poochy.

Plate 79

This impromptu portrait is of Mark Randall. It would have been a better shot but I was out with Amy when I saw Mark, and when I am out with Amy I am frequently under pressure. I get to play with my exposure settings only so long. Mark was once a neighborhood notable. He made a statement to the police and was interviewed on television not long after Luke Moore was reported missing. Apparently he was the last person in Portland to have seen Luke before his disappearance. He said he had seen him on the Saturday in question sitting alone in a booth at Mazatlan's. It was widely believed a credible sighting as Luke was known to have been inordinately fond of Mexican food. He is reported to have said on more than one occasion that if a thing couldn't be a pizza it should be a burrito or an enchilada—a sentiment with which most of us agreed wholeheartedly.

I have always liked hearing about how other people take their pictures. I am always hoping I might pick up some little something—something to emulate, something to avoid—that last little something I will need for the transformation from disgruntled hobbyist taking the sort of pictures he does to the presiding quasi-pro taking the sort of pictures he wants.

Unfortunately, I am not one of those photographers who can speak well about the experience of being a photographer. There aren't really many who can actually. Most of those who try seem to fall into one of two groups—self-promoting mystics or soulless technicians.

I like this particular picture for a number of reasons, not the least of which is its allusion to a dark, despairing, European sort of angst. There is a part of me that wishes I had indulged my inclination for this sort of thing a little more, but that part has been recalibrated with age and looks back on this regret with a bemused and slightly condescending affection.

Plate 81

I am, as you can see, definitely not an artist—I don't have a style, a subject, or a theory. I'm not even sure you would call me a photographer. I suppose you could call me an enthusiast, but I would rather you didn't as it is a heavily freighted tag crusted over with unsavory connotations. The cynic in me is tempted to say that the difference between these three—the enthusiast, the photographer, and the artist—is simple: a factor of 10 (or x10). An enthusiast sells a picture for $20, a photographer for $200, and an artist for $2000.

I bring this up because I was asked to sell a certain someone a copy of the above photo. It will decorate a dining room in Dayville.

Plate 82

The aerial shot—I have a weakness for them. I take as many as the acrophobic imperatives allow—dealing sometimes more successfully than others with that first glance down, that initial, self-preservational flush of adrenalin when I reflexively compute my falling velocity and estimate quasi-colonically the force and damage of my impact. I like the comprehensible overview, the greater understanding, the distance from actualities.

This particular shot was taken from a veranda on the sixteenth floor of the Federal Courthouse. It shows...well, you can see what it shows.

This photo is one of those that catches your attention right away. It has impact, but does it have staying power? No great photograph has the staying power of a great painting. No mediocre photograph has the staying power of a mediocre painting. It is only at the bottom of the barrel that things even out. Bad photos and bad paintings—the claims they make on one's attention are roughly equivalent.

This is the convenience store Tamara Grimshaw ran into when she tried to kill her husband—a photo of the ruined brick. It is a characterless shot. I have drained it as best I could of interest and feeling—not in reaction to a comparatively lush convention, but in deference to our judicial system and the mythic presumption of innocence. It is shot a little tighter than it should have been because, as you have no doubt noticed by now, I am not as a rule comfortable with a lot of negative space. I am not one of those managerially-approved sophisticates who trade in flavorless factualism, so you see very little here in the way of an empty parking lot. Sometimes these sorts of pictures—pictures of an impassive and emotionally arid urban landscape—can be a welcome relief from the endlessly replicating shots of a moody, cloud-crowned El Capitan, but they can't be a relief for long. Less is sometimes less. The law of diminishing returns is merciless (see Plate 71).

Plate 85

In photography if you pay attention, you will discover your tendencies over time. However much I admire nature or wildlife photography, I obviously do not do much of it myself. My interest is mainly in images that contain some sort of human element. Given my disposition, it should come as no surprise to discover that while I do both, my preference is for the artifact as opposed to the figure. For instance, the shot above. It is of Bill Hughes's helmet—the one he is required by law to wear every time he rides his ridiculous motorcycle—rather than of Bill Hughes himself.

Plate 86

I have a complicated reaction to Ryan Richardson—not just to his books, but to him personally. I both like him and am irritated by him. The strength of these competing feelings is influenced most directly by the frequency of our encounters. I like him best when I see him often or almost not at all. If I see him somewhere in between, some middling number of times within a certain period—neither a little or a lot—I become aware of certain annoying predispositions and am distracted from a full participation in the moment.

K. B. DIXON

This is a photo of Leah Ingram teaching her younger sister karate kicks out in their front yard. I was lucky to catch them in this illustrative juxtaposition. Leah has been taking self-defense classes at her father's insistence as part of her preparation for going off to college and, thoughtful sibling that she is, she has been passing on what she has learned to Gabrielle (Gabby). While there is something distinctly disturbing about the paramilitary mindset behind this enterprise, I can understand it. These are feral times we live in. Moral compasses are not what they used to be.

This picture relies heavily on the evocative power of the image to make its point. In other words, it is "romantic." I have no idea what it might mean to you, how you might use it—were you imaginatively so inclined—to illustrate some little story of your own about a singular place with magical powers, but for me it is a special piece of the past made palpable, an unusual feeling of metaphysical well-being given form.

     K. B. DIXON

Plate 89

I take a picture like this from time to time because I cannot help myself. As I would expect is quite obvious by now, I am attracted to images of absence and emptiness—this ostentatiously vacant street corner, for example (see also Plate 13). I got lucky here. The mix of summoned sensations—pleasant and unpleasant—has averaged out in favor of the thing.

Plate 90

Kayla is taking Omar to obedience school. She bought him a new collar for the occasion. She wanted him to feel confident on his first day. She let him choose. She says he showed a distinct preference for the traditional leather-with-buckle thing as opposed to the boring nylon slip.

She also gave him a bath so he would look and smell his best. ("There is no second chance to make a first impression.") Baths are not something Omar enjoys. The event invariably devolves into a game of wrestling match and chase.

K. B. DIXON

This is a photo of Paul Lewis, one of Portland's most famous photographers, at the opening of his new show at the Merrick Gallery. He is not one of my favorites. I have a hard time separating my dislike for him personally from my reaction to his pictures, which are, of course, always socially conscious and offered both thematically and chromatically in black and white. He was recently nominated for a Winfred Award by PPA (Portland Photographers Association) and used the occasion to advertise his virtue with a very public declining of it. He has been talking incessantly ever since about how disorienting the nomination was and what this sort of acceptance had done to his delicate, highly developed sensibility. He explained to anyone who would listen that he was simply not temperamentally prepared for this sort of success and adoration—a claim carefully designed, of course, to fortify his reputation and to gain him not only more success and adoration, but higher quality and longer-lasting success and adoration.

I have always been taken with the beauty of factual pho-tography. I like detail shots. I wish I could get Amy more interested in them. She is very dismissive of these sorts of pictures, finds them overly arty. They can be, but they don't have to be. She never gives them a chance. The above is a macro shot of a pinecone, its cloned crannies illuminated by a flashlight.

Plate 93

This is a picture of Terry Greenfield, Thomas Lockhart's assistant, sitting out in front of the courthouse on his lunch break. He is working a crossword puzzle. I have never understood the attraction of this sort of pointless intellection. I was using a 35mm prime when I took this picture, so I was close. It was snapped just before Terry asked me if I knew a nine-letter word that meant "disturbance." I offered "kerfuffle," a word I didn't even know I knew. I don't know where I picked it up. I have never used it in a sentence. I can't imagine that I ever would.

A group shot is not an easy thing. This one is of the derelicts I play poker with. We would like to give ourselves a name, but we haven't come up with a good one yet. We are still working on it. Gary Farrell, the man in front with the ridiculous haircut and wearing the actual suspenders, owes me $5 from last night. We will see how long it takes him to pay up. He is notoriously slow. (I have a bet with Carl Lane, the guy in the back row, second from the right. He says two weeks; I say four.) Gary is always cash-strapped. He has been spending a lot of money on marriage counseling. His wife, Laura, is at this very moment sprawled languorously beside a pool in Cabo. She is one of those people who likes to spend as much time as she can in the sun. I suspect even her insides are tan.

Plate 95

Garbage day. 6 p.m. Wide-angle shot down a well-appointed alleyway. The natives are arriving home from work, gathering up their cans and their recycling bins. The small congregation out behind the Iversons started as a single pair of chatty neighbors. They were joined by another pair, then another pair, then another until we ended up with the gaggle you see. The conversation—such as it was—drifted for a while from subject to subject (weather, lawn maintenance, HOA fees) coming to rest at last on the Moores, who apparently had not set anything out for pickup this morning. They were, it seems, recreating perfunctorily in the San Juans. (The Riddles look after their place when they are gone.) The tete-a-tete moved from the Moores' whereabouts to missing Luke's. There was, of course, considerable speculation about just what had happened. Most seemed to think Luke had simply run away. They expected he would be found hiding out in San Francisco with an older woman. She would have a tattoo. There was debate about what this tattoo might be of and where it might be located—and if it would or would not have been done in good taste. Everyone was certain that drugs would be involved.

Initially there was sympathy for the Moores—for Daniel and Rebecca— when it was thought to be possible some sort of heinousness had happened, but that began to change as

the accumulating evidence started to suggest that heinousness might not be the issue. People started to think of them
more or less unsympathetically—as everyday solipsists
whose parenting skills were significantly below average.

 K. B. DIXON

Plate 96

This is a photo I took of Ryan Richardson giving an interview—a thing he does not like to do, is terrible at, and avoids whenever he can. His discomfort is palpable. This particular interview was with Sara Kinman, the spindly press rep for a small foundation that had selected Ryan as a finalist for their fiction award this year. As I took this shot he was discussing, or trying to discuss, Helmer's Hat Shop. It is difficult (maybe impossible) to find a Ryan Richardson book that does not mention Helmer's Hat Shop—or Haberdashery. The point of these shout-outs seems to shift. When asked about them Ryan invariably hems and haws and will make no definitive avowals. I like the way the light reflects off the psychic sweat that is glazing his furrowed brow.

I have tried as much as possible to avoid political pictures—
photos that allude to the villainy of various imperfect soci-
eties. From time to time I have instead chosen to take pictures that allude to the villainy of imperfect individuals. I
have simply never cared for politics in my art—I don't like
it in painting, I don't like it in literature, I don't like it in
movies, I don't like it in photography.

K. B. DIXON

Kayla is testing new dog foods. She wants the best and brightest involved in Omar's dinner. She has been reading up on metabolizable energy. She knows everything there is to know about protein requirements, mineral supplements, and beet pulp.

You will notice that with a slight tilt I have once again intro-
duced a diagonal and that I have once again broken the frame
with it. (I am starting to think of this as a trick.) The young
lady you see with Rachael Lockhart is Mia Berry—John and
Julie's brilliant and ornately dimpled daughter. Mia's mother—
the just-mentioned Julie (a bit dimpled herself)—is for the
most part a nice enough woman, but she seems constitution-
ally incapable of having any kind of conversation that does
not include a lavish tribute to academic achievement and an
allusory reference to the scholarship offers that are about to
begin raining down on her darling little descendant. There is
something almost ritualistic about these incantations, these
oblique, mantra-like flourishes, that suggests they might
serve some sort of occult function for Julie—be some sort of
nonbeliever's substitute for prayer. Her husband for his part
speaks only of the girl's athletic prowess, her prodigaic way
with a tennis racquet, her courageous attitude toward perspi-
ration. He is an odd-looking man—John Berry. He combs his
hair straight back for a sleek, aerodynamic look. In conversation he has a weakness for hypotheticals, which, of course,
I do not. (My lack of interest in them stems directly from
my inability to deal with what is actual. I can see no value
in moving the locus of my incomprehension from what is to
what might have been or could be.)

Plate 100

Is photography art? This was apparently a question for debate until just recently. According to the professoriate the question has been answered in the affirmative by institutional consensus. Personally I am not so sure. (I am also not so sure it actually matters.) That photography has had the title conferred on it is obviously true, but with contemporary curatorial silliness running the polished hallways of power unchecked, the authority of these institutions to make this conferment has been rightly called into question. I know photographers would like it to be considered "art," would like to have their names decorated with the designation, but it seems to me an overly broad use of the word. Referring to a photographer as an "artist" is like referring to a musician as one; it may be loosely accurate, but it doesn't really seem to be strictly the case. The appellation seems more a complex species of honorifica than a statement of fact. I would, of course, prefer to feel some other way about all of this (as I have a knee-jerk reaction to any conservative impulse), but I don't. I am just going to have to sit tight for a while and wait for a face-saving transformation.

For all of its attraction, there is a quality to some street photography that I have a little trouble with: its unrelieved earnestness. I can take this occasionally like cough syrup and benefit, but too much of it upsets my stomach. I prefer my pictures a little less sanctimonious, my photographers a little less certain of their own good intentions and privileged access to the truth.

As far as I am concerned, the above is a simple shot of character, not circumstance. It makes no claim on the social documentary for which I have some sympathy as a consumer of photography, but in which I have no interest whatsoever as a producer of photography.

Plate 102

Above is an exterior shot of the Thoresen Gallery. Below is a list of words that appeared in an extended review of the show inside—a show I liked very much:

thematic

geographical

subsumed

interpretive

manifested

revealing

rigorous

equivalent

trajectory

diverse

mediating

cacophony

signage

disembodied

immerse

examination

ephemeral

participate

unleashed

urgency

juxtaposition

Stairs. I would like to take more pictures of them, but as a subject they seem to me for the most part worn out so I limit myself to the stray indulgence. When I give way to the inclination as I have here, the question immediately becomes one of direction—should I shoot them from the top down or the bottom up. Graphically I prefer to shoot from the top down. It is easier to accentuate the geometry. Emotionally, philosophically, and metaphorically I prefer to shoot from the bottom up to underline their allusive qualities, their reference to the Sisyphean struggle, to suffering, to the arduousness of living.

Plate 104

Kayla spent the morning teaching Omar to read—or so she
claimed.

I think of my pictures as thoughtful, generally coherent, and responsive, but rarely as passionate. For me passion is usually a pander, the hobgoblin of the self-aggrandizing school. I don't mind it so much and, in fact, am often moved by it in photojournalistic work, but in fine-art stuff it is gravel in my granola, the first refuge of the scoundrel. I know I am supposed to be a little more generous in my sentiments here, more ecumenical, and I wish I were. I would enjoy the way it would make me feel about myself, but that just doesn't seem to be a good enough reason to pretend.

Plate 106

Sometimes when you look at a picture you think about all of the other ones you could have taken at that same moment but didn't—closer, farther away, different angle. You don't know why you chose this one over that one. There are intuitive twitches, semi-conscious reasons, cowardly allegiances to expediency. This particular shot of the Taylor house was taken at 1 a.m. I was set up on the sidewalk with a tripod. It was still as always—the creepy quiet disturbed only by the chirping of crickets and the tisk, tisk, tisking of automated sprinkler systems. As you can see, the lights are on at the Taylors. They are always on—or they have been ever since Susan's husband Greg moved out. That was two years ago. Susan has distracted herself from this abandonment with late-night television and hobbies—she birdwatches and gossips. She has become the neighborhood bulletinboard busying herself with everyone else's business. She trades information freely on her regular patrols—her morning, afternoon, and evening walks—and at the center coffee shop. Unfortunately for those involved in these trades, Susan is a pudgy person, a dieter—a dedicated and adventurous one who finds the subject of weight-loss interesting and thinks everyone else does as well. If you really want to know just exactly what it is the Herzingers are planning to do with that god-awful orange patio awning, you will first have to listen to a lengthy lecture on trans fats.

Plate 107

This water-feature does not do nearly what the developers of this massive complex hoped it would—in part because it is conceptually uninspired, but mostly because it has not been fully committed to. It is, as you can see, proportionally underwhelming—an earring on an elephant. Still, I suppose one must grudgingly admit it is better than nothing. I have shot the trifling waterfall in a contrarian style—that is, I have frozen the water in place with a fast shutter speed. The how-to books on shooting waterfalls advocate relentlessly for the silky-flow effect as the professional's grail, the universally preferred and revered objective. They offer up the secret for getting it as if it were the formula for a cancer cure (filters and shutter speeds of 1 to 2 seconds). This effect is, however, exactly the one I did not want. I have never liked anything about it. An effect that looks like an effect is rarely of much interest, and this one—the silky-moving-water one—seems to me to be an especially stale example of reflexive romanticism.

K. B. DIXON

Plate 108

I took this picture a year ago of Daniel Moore walking his ridiculous little dog Nano. I was trying out my new zoom lens. It is here to compare with the photo below.

I took this picture of Daniel walking out to his car (which for some reason he had parked in his driveway and not in his garage) approximately a week after his son Luke disappeared. I was trying to catch something, but didn't—which makes this, in essence, a photo of something you can't quite see. What I was trying to catch was Daniel's transformed carriage. It was one thing before Luke went missing and another thing after. There is now a slight, sort of mournful sag to him—as if his vertebrae had been slightly compressed by the weight of his worry. He feels significant in a way he did not before.

Kayla went with Omar to a Halloween party. As you can see, they wore matching capes and hats. Sarah watched me take this shot. "This could be the start of something," she said. "Something sorta Arbus-y."

Plate 110

This photo was taken by my friend, the writer Ryan Richardson. He showed it to me the other day. He wanted my opinion. I told him that I liked it, but I was not a professional—I was an amateur.

The woman in the baggy pants and sunglasses standing behind the bicycle (which you will notice has not only a basket, but a pair of saddlebags and a bell) is Melissa Richardson, Ryan's wife. She is an anxiety-ridden eccentric so, of course, we got on from the beginning. I remember a long talk with her once about perception—about the way people think about other people. It fascinated her the way we so often allow single facts to serve as full descriptions. For instance, if this or that person knew you as detached, pessimistic, or controlled, they would assume you could not be sentimental, confident, or impulsive—that being detached, pessimistic, or controlled somehow precluded your being sentimental, confident, or impulsive when, in fact, you might very well have been those things because, like most people, you were a composite of contradictions and incompatibilities. Some possibilities might be excluded because of this or that quality, but certainly not nearly as many as one might reasonably expect.

This is another one of my Portland, Inside and Out pictures—an homage to Eugene Atget. I am a big fan of his. For all the attention given his pictures of an old, peopleless Paris, it is his peopleless Parisian interiors and storefronts that I think I like the best. Photography was for him what I have said before it is for many (myself included)—a refuge from artistic incompetency, the place to go when you couldn't paint. In Atget's case it was also apparently the place to go when you couldn't act.

K. B. DIXON

I think of this landscape as one of my Klines. He is some-thing of a local legend—Gary Kline—a card-carrying member of the pretty-picture school of photography. He and his buddies (a bearded gaggle of Ansel Adams wan-nabes) have produced a never-ending stream of spectacular postcards. They seem to offer more workshops than images these days. They appear to take a special pleasure in refer-ring to themselves as artists. Maybe they are—but if this is so, I would have to say they are not important ones.

Providence Hospital. There is nothing more depressing than walking into this building or more invigorating than walking out. There is no color in the spectrum more devastating than gauze-white.

Plate 114

I have included this picture—the yellow-arrowed entrance to a parking garage—because I liked it so much. It turned out the way I wanted it to and awakened in me a hope for the future, a hope that tomorrow I might take another picture that was similarly satisfying.

Kayla is planning a trip to the mountains. She wants Omar to see snow. She wants him to have a wild, primal, wolfish experience. She wants him to have the chance at least once in his life to chase a rabbit.

K. B. DIXON

Plate 116

The Achilles heel of my imagery is brightness. When it comes to saturation and contrast, we agree. But brightness—well, I like less. This might have changed if I had not just taken that picture of Dr. Huffman's door but gone through it and opened myself up to his compassionate dispensations.

Plate 117

This is a shot of Christopher Welch. He works in that tall glassy new building downtown. I don't know what he does for a living, just that it is the sort of thing that is done in a building like that—the sort of thing that requires a nice suit, a good haircut, and an unfeigned interest in high finance.

Christopher is a dedicated and zealous hand-shaker. He puts a lot of energy and grip into it—the idea being to make a peremptorily forceful declaration of hairy-chested manliness. I can't recall having ever liked anyone who went in for this sort of thing. I have tried to get a picture of him administering this crushing, caveman clasp, but haven't yet.

Plate 118

As I have said before, I do not like trying to capture motion in a picture, but time—time is always there. It is, in fact, this temporal element that invariably draws me to the medium—the image as a ghost, the arrested specter of the present just past, a thing already on its way to becoming history. What will the above street scene look like to me in thirty years—the brickwork, the advertisements?

A person, a place, a thing—for me a picture is always a picture of time, an instant rescued from oblivion.

Painting is considerably harder than photography, but thinking about painting is easier.

 K. B. DIXON

Kayla is letting Omar choose his own Christmas present. To me he looks confused.